Elements of Change

Elements of Change

KEYNIN CARL BATTLE

PALMETTO
P U B L I S H I N G
Charleston, SC
www.PalmettoPublishing.com

Copyright © 2024 by Keynin Carl Battle

All rights reserved
No portion of this book may be reproduced, stored in a retrieval system, or transmitted in any form by any means–electronic, mechanical, photocopy, recording, or other– except for brief quotations in printed reviews, without prior permission of the author.

Hardcover ISBN: 9798822960534
Paperback ISBN: 9798822960541

CHAPTER 1

Summoning

Keith Cottom was a twenty-two-year-old cashier at a local grocery store. He was a hard worker, always there when he was needed, and his manager always appreciated his hard work and effort. After returning from work, he was alone in his apartment; he felt trapped in a cycle. One night while he was walking home, he wished the world was more magical and every day was a new adventure.

In the mix of making dinner, something strange happened. A circle with strange symbols appeared under him, then a bright light engulfed him. When the light faded and he opened his eyes, he was surrounded by an elf, a troll, a goblin, a lizardman, a dwarf, a fairy, a vampire, and a demon.

In shock and fear, he said, "Where am I, and who are you people?"

The male elf approached Keith with a friendly smile and explained why he was summoned there. A long time ago when their world was new, six powerful cosmic spirits came to this world and enchanted it with their power. Each spirit had their own element; there was the spirit of water, the spirit of earth, the spirit of fire, the spirit of wind, the spirit of light, and the spirit of darkness. Soon every race had the spirits' magic that they used for everyday life.

One day, an evil being emerged from the darkness, claiming he would conquer and enslave this world. He recruited two demons, an elf, a lizardman, and a vampire, enhancing their power with his darkness and turning them into dark versions of themselves. The name of this dark lord was Valac, the elder lich. With the help of his army of undead and his five generals, he enslaved this world and its citizens. All hope was lost, and everyone lived in fear, until one person from each race came together and combined their light magic to perform a summoning. They were surprised and shocked it worked; they summoned the first human in this world. For a few months, they taught him how to use magic, and he had a plan to defeat Lord Valac. Lord Valac and his army were travelling through the land when a cloud of smoke came out of nowhere. His undead dropped like flies, and his generals chased the summoners, leaving Lord Valac to face off with the human.

Lord Valac said, "I will kill you and those who have summoned you."

The human replied, "We will never submit to a monster like you!"

An epic battle took place, and when it looked like the human was about to die, he activated his trap. A ring of light surrounded him. When Valac's generals heard his scream, they rushed to help him, but all they did was get trapped too. The magic the human used was light magic, which seals those with high darkness magic in them. The human opened a portal to a realm of darkness before sending Valac and his generals into it.

Lord Valac said, "I will return and turn everyone into my army of the undead."

He replied, "You should feel at home there. It's as dark as your heart, and if you do come back, another human like me will defeat you."

After Valac and his generals were sealed away, light returned to this world. The human spent the remainder of his life helping the eight races rebuild their world. Then in each country, they built schools to help everyone learn how to use their magic. Since the human they summoned was in his twenties, all students were required to be twenty to enroll. When the human was on his deathbed, all the rulers of the races came to thank him. He had one request before he died.

"Every new school year when a human dies, please summon a new human, and teach him how to use his magic."

For one thousand years, they honored his request, and now Keith Cottam had been chosen.

CHAPTER 2

A New Beginning

Keith felt sad that he had to leave his friends, family, and old life behind, but he was excited and thrilled about his new life in this world. The headmasters introduced themselves. The elf's name was Horith, the troll was Hugo, the goblin Weilt, the lizardman Vaxl, the dwarf Ugran, the fairy Krystal, the vampire Viktor, and the demon was Leonard.

Keith introduced himself. "Hello, I'm Keith Cottam, and I'm excited to be here."

Horith toured Keith around the school; it was like a combination of a castle and college campus. Then he was introduced to his homeroom teacher, a fairy named Iris Meadow. After meeting his teacher, Horith gave him written instructions on how to find his dorm room. Keith was shocked he didn't know this writing, but he could understand it.

Horith told him, "It's a gift for coming to this world."

Keith now could read, write, speak, and understand their language. Before Horith left, he told Keith to come to the student hall for student orientation first thing in the morning.

Walking toward his dorm, Keith was hit with a strong wind spell. A beautiful woman with silver-white hair and ruby-red eyes approached him. Keith stared in awe. She saw he was bleeding from his cheek and offered her handkerchief. After smelling his blood, she bit down on his neck without thinking. She pulled away and apologized for biting him. Keith rubbed his neck and asked if she was a vampire. She replied with a yes and said her name was Catherine Rodante.

Keith asked in a worried voice, "Now that you've bitten me, will I become a vampire too?"

Catherine covered her mouth and laughed, saying, "What are you talking about? Vampires aren't made. They're born like normal."

Keith apologized and explained who he was and why he asked that. Catherine explained why she hit him with her wind magic; she was practicing and lost focus. After saying goodbye, Keith headed straight to his dorm room and went straight to sleep once his head hit the pillow. Before drifting off to sleep, he was nervous and excited to see what other people and things await him in this world.

CHAPTER 3

The Duel

At orientation in the hall, every race lined up in a row, but Keith, being the only human, was in the center between the goblins and the trolls. A handsome blond elf walked onstage and gave a speech.

"Hello and welcome, old and new students. I'm Elaith Undomiel, the student president of the school of magic. I'm so pleased to see so many new students here, and so you know, this is my last year here, and I must choose five candidates to take my place as the next president. So work and study hard because the next president could be you. Now before we head to class, there's someone here that I'd love to hear from. Can Keith Cottam please come onstage?"

Keith took the stage, and the students looked at him with awe and interest, but others looked angry and disgusted. Elaith asked Keith to tell everyone how he was feeling and a little about himself.

Keith said, "Hello, I'm Keith Cottam. I'm excited to learn magic and make some new friends. My hobbies are listening to music, watching old movies, hiking, and hanging out at my favorite diner."

There was quiet applause, but Keith was happy to see Catherine. Keith walked to Mrs. Meadow's homeroom and sat right next to Catherine. During class, Mrs. Meadow explained to her class how magic worked.

"It's all about visualization," she said. "You must picture the element and what you want it to do."

Mrs. Meadow asked Keith to come up and give it a try. Keith focused on his image and created a big ball of water. Everyone was amazed, but when Keith lost focus, the ball exploded and everyone got wet.

At lunch, Keith sat at a table alone; it reminded him how alone he was in his own life until a goblin named Noah Withering and a lizardman named Zosk Mudwood came over. They asked to sit with him; he said yes. Catherine sat right next to Keith. He felt happy for the first time. He made friends in school.

A troll came behind Keith and grabbed him by the collar and threw him against the wall. Noah and Zosk rushed to him, but Catherine was stopped by the troll; she pushed him away. Noah used his light magic to heal his injuries.

Keith talked to his friends about his world and learned more about his friends. Noah was from a family of merchants, Zosk was the son of the lizard chief, and Catherine was a daughter of a noble family. He said good night to his friends and headed straight to bed.

In the morning after Keith met his friends, the troll from the day before came up to him and said, "I, Jord Dunker, challenge you to a magic duel."

Everyone stared and gasped as Jord challenged Keith. One of the headmasters, Viktor, came up and insisted Keith accept the challenge. Keith accepted the challenge, then the headmaster asked him to come to his office. Viktor explained what the magic duels were and what they were for. The magic duel was a way for students to test and improve their magic. The headmasters and teachers observed their students. It was also a way for someone to get their name out; the winner of the duel would be announced across the lands so village leaders, nobles, and royals could hear about them.

After leaving Viktor's office, Keith found his friends were waiting outside to talk to him. They told him about Jord and what to expect. Jord was top of his class and an expert in fire magic. Jord's powerful attacks were fire blast and flame whirlwind. To help Keith feel prepared, each of his friends offered to help him. Catherine showed him how to use wind magic to move fast and block and reflect attacks. Noah taught him how to use light magic to blind his opponent, and Zosk taught him earth magic to create rock bullets and walls. With the help of his friends, Keith felt confident and ready for his duel.

Keith and Jord's duel was about to begin. Students, teachers, the student council, and some reporters came to watch the match. The gong rang. Jord launched a fireball, but Keith dodged it with the wind magic he'd learned. A giant wall of fire surrounded Keith; he was losing air, so he had to think fast. Like on the first day of class, Keith created a giant ball of water and exploded it. The wall was gone, and he could think straight. Jord launched another fireball at him, but it was a water reflection of himself. Keith trapped Jord in a mirror maze. Jord fired in every direction, but all he was doing was wasting his magic and energy before Keith's final attack. He blasted Jord with light magic to blind him, then used his water magic to blast him up like a geyser. Once he landed, Keith used earth magic to bind his hands and feet. Students and teachers applauded and cheered for him.

The student president smiled and said to himself, "That was an impressive duel. That human…no, Keith Cottam has amazing skills."

The headmasters took Keith to the grand office where he was summoned from to reward him with fifty thousand gold coins. They explained to Keith that gold coins were this world's currency. Students earned them by helping in school or with the magic duel. They could help teachers with their projects, run errands, and work in the cafeteria. The duel was a way to double their earnings, but losing cut their money in half. Keith started with twenty thousand gold coins; now it was fifty thousand. He was also given five hundred coins for his impressive magic skills. From that duel, Keith made 50,500 coins. From what he learned, one gold was ten dollars from his world, so he made 550,000 dollars. He thanked his headmasters and retired to his room.

In the morning at the yard, students surrounded him. The male students said he was amazing and cool, and the females said he was handsome and very talented. He pushed through the crowd and met up with his friends. Keith wasn't interested in popularity or having fans; all he wanted was wonderful friends, and he found that with Catherine, Noah, and Zosk.

Keith's victory spread across the country to the leaders of their kingdoms. In the land of lizard folk, Chief Skinks said, "This human was just summoned here, and yet he adapted quickly to his new environment. Quite impressive."

In the land of goblins, King Mogglewog said with a smile, "It's about time someone put that brat in his place. King Ymer must be furious."

In the land of trolls, King Ymer said angrily, "How dare that human do this to my third son! Now all the rulers will think we're weak. Just you wait. I'll make that human regret he was summoned here."

In the land of vampires, King Vladamir said, "This is the first time in years that a human made headlines. This Keith Cottam has some unique skills."

Queen Ambrosia replied, "Yes, my darling. You know, our niece happens to go to that school with him. I hope we get to meet him."

In the land of dwarves, King Azaghal laughed and said, "That Keith's got talent. The last human our school summoned two hundred years ago couldn't hit the side of a barn."

In the land of fairies, King Oberon said with a smile, "This Keith really caught my eye; I wonder if he would be interested in marrying one of my two daughters."

In the land of demons, Queen Hecate said with a mysterious smile, "Well, well, well, this human is quite fascinating. I wonder if he would be interested in being the ruler of demons."

CHAPTER 4

The Transfer Demon

On his way to class, Keith smelled something sweet in the air. He saw a demon girl with little horns being bullied by a bunch of elf girls. He jumped in between them, protecting the demon girl.

With anger, he shouted, "Stop this! Leave her alone now."

They ran off. He gently touched her shoulder, then looked at the demon and asked if she was ok. She nodded. He picked up her basket, and inside were a dozen muffins. He took a bite of one of them, and it was delicious. Without thinking, Keith devoured every one of them. Keith rubbed his tummy, licked his lips, and smiled with satisfaction. Keith looked at the empty basket with shock and worry. He gave her basket back and apologized.

She said, "No, it's ok. I don't mind that you ate them all. I'm just concerned because they fell on the ground."

Keith replied, "Oh, they only fell on the grass. They weren't dirty at all," he said with a smile. Keith gasped. He was going to be late. He said goodbye and ran off. Keith's friends asked why he was almost late, but before he could answer, class started. Mrs. Meadow announced that a new transfer student would be joining this class.

She came in the room and introduced herself. "Hi, I'm Lulu Infernus from the land of demons."

Keith realized it was the girl he saved.

She smiled, rushed over, hugged him, and said with joy, "Oh, it's you. I'm so happy we're in the same class."

After Keith's other class was over, he headed to the cafeteria to see his friends. Once again, Keith saw Lulu being bullied. They were saying mean things to her and were going to hurt her with magic. Keith created an earth wall to protect her.

He said, "I thought I told you to leave her alone."

One of the bullies said, "Oh, look. The succubus seduced the human to be her bodyguard."

Keith looked at Lulu with confusion; she looked down to the ground with sadness. Headmaster Ugran came out of nowhere and asked what was going on. The girls said they were being friendly, but Keith said they were bullying Lulu and threatening to hurt her. Ugran whistled, and an owl landed on his arm. He asked it who was telling the truth. The owl pointed at Keith, and Ugran told the girls to come to his office.

Keith asked Lulu if she was ok, but she was crying. He asked what was wrong, and she explained that she was just happy someone was very kind to her. Keith asked if she would like to join him and his friends for lunch. She said yes and held his arm. Noah, Zosk, and Catherine saw Lulu clinging on his arm. Catherine looked jealous. Keith explained what happened. They all sat down and had lunch together.

CHAPTER 5

The Date and Princess

In combination class, Professor Thorin, the dwarf, explained how to use combo magic. He explained that combining two different elements would create something new, like fire and wind made lightning, fire and water made mist, earth and fire made metal, water and earth made wood, wind and earth made sand, and water and wind made ice.

On his way out, Keith ran into Lulu, and she asked him on a date. Before he could answer, Catherine jumped in and asked to come with them.

Lulu said, "Of course, you're more than welcome to come on our date." She explained that Keith should be surrounded by a whole group of girls.

Keith's and Catherine's faces turned red, and Keith said, "Well, I gotta go, but I'll see you two tomorrow at the front gate."

At the gate, Keith saw Lulu and Catherine waiting. They both looked lovely. Lulu took his arm, and Catherine took the other arm. They took a bus-like carriage pulled by a giant dragon to town. The elves' town was beautiful with stone buildings and wooden stands. Keith asked why there were so many elves but no others here. The girls explained that this world was split into eight factions, one for each race. The reason the magic schools had so many races was because each headmaster from each race hand selected students to enroll.

On their date, they watched a play about the human who defeated Lord Valac. When the play was over, Keith felt invigorated and proud that he was summoned to this world. Lulu took Keith and Catherine to a nice place for lunch in the red-light district. Beautiful and seductive elf women were standing behind glass windows. Keith and Catherine were very uncomfortable. Lulu said there was a nice little café that they were going to love. Little did they know that in the sewers, some demons were performing a dark ritual.

They were chanting in a strange language, and the demon in the center said, "Oh, Lord Valac, I ask you to infuse me with darkness so I can free you and become the most powerful demon in the world."

A group of elves attacked the demons, but as they interrupted the ritual, the darkness turned the demon in the center into a wild, out-of-control monster. It burst out of the sewer in front of Keith, Lulu, and Catherine. Citizens began to run and scream as the monster went on a rampage. Keith realized he had to do something. He blasted a fireball at it, then used air magic to fly away and lure it away from the elves. The monster had skin like steel; no matter how many attacks Keith threw, the creature seemed impenetrable. Lulu and Catherine managed to discombobulate the monster long enough to come up with a plan.

Keith lured the monster to the center of town, used sand to blind it in a sandstorm, made metal spikes to impale it, and created an ice dome to surround it. Finally Lulu used her fire magic, combining it with Catherine's wind magic to create lightning to explode the monster. The citizens cheered for them. Elf soldiers came to them and asked them to accompany them to the castle.

Inside the castle, they were greeted by the ruler of the elves, Princess Gemstarzah Aeglin. She was beautiful with golden blond hair and sapphire-blue eyes.

The princess said, "Keith Cottam, you performed a noble deed, defeating that evil monster and keeping my people safe. I reward you with my hand in marriage."

The royal council gasped and muttered to each other. Keith was flabbergasted, Catherine looked furious, and Lulu looked happy and encouraged Keith to accept her offer. The royal adviser, Iorhael, told the princess that this was too far of an advance and asked Keith what he wanted for a reward.

Keith thought about it and said, "I do not require any grand reward. What I really want is to improve my magic and learn more about this world because I was summoned to this world to protect it, so I want to learn all I can, because knowledge is true power."

Everyone was surprised and astounded by his request.

Princess Galadriel said, "I like you even more. In fact, I grant you access to the royal library and reward you and your friends with one hundred thousand gold coins each."

They accepted her offer and headed back to school.

CHAPTER 6

Familiars

Keith told Noah and Zosk what happened on his date.
Zosk said, "Wow, sounds like you had quite a date."
Noah said, "You are quite the charmer. First, those two, now the princess. Maybe you can give me some pointers. There's this elf guy I've got my eyes on."
Keith nervously laughed and said, "Oh, we better get outside for our next class."
Mrs. Divna, a demon, was teaching her class familiar summoning. Headmaster Ugran was there, too, with his owl Ajax to explain what familiars were and their uses.

"They are life partners who help improve your magic and become your eyes and ears in the world. To summon them, you combine your light magic and dark magic, close your eyes, and in your head, call out to your familiar. Once your familiar comes to you, let them taste your blood and give them a name to seal your pact."

One by one, students started to summon their familiars. Noah summoned a slime, Zosk summoned a salamander, Lulu summoned an imp, and Catherine summoned a fox. Now it was Keith's turn. He concentrated on his light and darkness magic. Without warning, a loud howl came out of the shadow; it was a shadow wolf. It looked dangerous. The teachers ordered all students to stay back—but not Keith. He stayed still and offered his hand.

In a calm and soft voice, he said, "It's ok. You're just scared. You're somewhere you don't know surrounded by strange people. I know. I was just like you."

The wolf calmed down. Keith bit his thumb and dropped his blood on the wolf. Keith named him Ash. Ash licked Keith's face with joy. Everyone was amazed that Keith tamed and forged a pact with a shadow wolf. For the rest of the day, the students trained and bonded with their familiars. Noah trained his slime, named Sloop, to manipulate all the elements. Zosk combined his earth magic with the fire of his salamander, Vulcanus, to create weapons. With the help of Lulu's imp, Blaze, Lulu's fire magic got stronger. Catherine's fox, Kitsune, sharpened her focus on her magic and surroundings. Keith was testing Ash's shadow magic; Ash could move through the shadows. Whenever Keith didn't need Ash, he retreated into his shadow.

CHAPTER 7

My Little Devil Sister

Professor Wendigo was teaching his class about wood magic and how it connected everyone to their world.

"When we combine our earth and water magic to the trees, we can see how they grew and their surroundings." Professor Wendigo told his students to go deep into the forest and to connect to the oldest tree they could find.

Keith used his wind magic to fly deep into the forest, but then he heard a scream and went to investigate it. When he landed, he saw a little demon girl with short brown hair and little curly goat horns surrounded by giant bat creatures. He used wind to cut off their wings and earth bullets to finish them. The girl looked frightened, so Keith offered some candy he bought at a store in town. She loved it, and Keith asked for her name.

She said in a soft voice, "Olivia."

A few feet away was a wagon in a complete wreck and two demon bodies. Keith used earth magic to give them a proper resting place, then Keith gave Olivia two flowers and told her to put each one on their graves.

She cried, and Keith said, "I'm so sorry for your loss, but I promise I will take care of you from now on."

Keith used wind magic to take her to Professor Wendigo. He told him the situation. Professor Wendigo told him to take her to the headmasters where they would decide what should be done with her. They decided to send her to an orphanage, but Olivia clutched Keith's arm, and Keith promised he would take care of her. The headmasters prohibited this. It was against school rules for students of the opposite sex to live together.

Keith asked, "Do students have to live in the dorms, or do they have their own place to live?"

They said, "No, students have their own homes."

So Keith decided to buy his own house so he could take care of Olivia. The headmasters approved of this; Keith got an excuse to leave the rest of his classes to look for a house. Keith found a beautiful house a few miles outside of school. It had an upstairs with three bedrooms, a big living room, a kitchen, and a big yard next to a forest. Ash and Olivia ran across the yard with joy. Olivia hugged Keith and thanked him for all he had done.

Keith happily said, "I'm really happy I found you. Without family, I felt alone in this world, but with you here, I feel like I'm taking care of a little sister, so from now on, we're family."

At dusk, all of Keith's friends came over to throw a housewarming party for him and Olivia. There was also a surprise visit from Princess Gemstarzah. They gave gifts to Olivia, mostly clothes and toys. At the end, everyone left. Gemstarzah insisted on staying the night, but her adviser came for her. Olivia was fast asleep on the couch, so Keith picked her up and took her to her bed.

CHAPTER 8

The Fairy Godmother

Before Keith left for school, he ate breakfast with Olivia and prepared lunch for her to eat later. Ash stayed behind to guard the house and Olivia. Keith flew to school. In the middle of class, Keith constantly worried about Olivia being alone. At lunch with his friends, Keith decided to hire a housemaid to look after Olivia when he was at school. Noah suggested he go to a slave market since they had a great variety of people to choose from.

On their day off from school, they went to the market. Keith was nervous to go in; he was expecting to see sad, beat up, and scarred slaves with raggedy old cloth for clothes. Once they went inside, he saw it was bright and clean, and the slaves had clean and proper clothes and true smiles. The owner was a vampire named Rosa Alvarenga who asked how she could help them. Keith asked for someone who could clean and cook and also someone who could teach reading, writing, and math to Olivia. She showed him Violet, the fifth child of a poor family who sold their children.

"She's the last of her siblings here," Rosa said. "All of them were sold to be servants, handmaids, and concubines. While she was here, her reading, writing, and math skills improved exponentially."

After asking Violet a few more questions, he decided to buy her. Keith signed some papers and was given the key to her collar. After leaving the market, Keith removed her collar. Violet looked confused and asked why.

Keith said, "I don't like the idea of you as a slave. I would like to hire you, and I promise if you work hard, I will pay you thirty gold coins a week."

She cried and thanked him for his kindness. The girls took Violet shopping for essentials, and the guys bought food to throw a welcome party for her. At Keith's house, everyone was there. Olivia gave Violet a bouquet of flowers she picked to welcome her. Ash wagged his tail and licked her face.

A few weeks had passed since Keith hired Violet, and she was doing a wonderful job. She was doing great with cooking, cleaning, laundry, and shopping. Olivia's reading, writing, and math skills improved thanks to her. Violet was a wonderful member of Keith's new family.

CHAPTER 9

The Festival

Before class started, a message came through wooden speakers on the wall. It was a type of wind magic that channeled the user's voice into a louder volume across the room. The announcement was about the elf festival for spring. When spring was here, the elves threw a festival to thank the spirits for blessing this world.

The townspeople were all preparing for the festival. Streamers of flowers were being hung, smells of fresh-baked bread and sweets flooded the air, and children were playing and singing with joy. All the students were given tasks to help with the festival. President Elaith gave Keith a task to help make wine. Keith saw a bunch of people stomping on grapes in large, wide buckets. After cleaning his feet, he started stomping on grapes. He had a hard time finding his rhythm, and some others were having trouble until he had an idea. Keith pulled out his MP3 player and looked for a song with a good beat. Using wind magic, he channeled the sound to travel all around so everyone could hear it. The song he chose was "Come and Get Your Love" by Redbone. The words were foreign to everyone, but they loved the sound and rhythm. They started to turn into a dance troupe. At the end, they made more wine than they thought. Everyone thanked Keith for his help.

Keith was exhausted, but at home, a nice hot dinner was waiting for him. Keith was so happy to have dinner with Violet and Olivia. A wave of nostalgia hit him—memories of eating dinner with his family back when he was younger. After he was living on his own, he barely saw his family, but now thanks to Olivia and Violet, he got it back.

Before going to bed, Keith said, "Thanks, you two. I completely forgot what eating with family felt like. So let's keep making more memories like this."

With a hug, Olivia replied, "I feel the same, big brother. Let's keep making more memories."

Violet said, "I'm so happy to hear that, Sir Cottam. I'm so grateful to work for you."

A few days later, the festival began. Keith, Olivia, Violet, and all his friends explored the festival. There was food, music, and games. Catherine and Lulu offered Keith food. Zosk was checking out the weapon venue, Noah was playing the archery game, and Olivia and Violet were exploring more of the festival. An elf woman approached Olivia and asked her if she would like to enter the flower girl pageant. It was a contest where little girls created their own flower crowns and showed them to the audience.

Keith and his friends watched the pageant. There were a bunch of elves, some fairies, and a few vampires onstage. Olivia was next, and she looked so cute with her flower crown and two little ones on her horns. The winner of the contest was Olivia. The crowd cheered, and her prize was she could take one of the stuffed cosmic spirits toys home with her. She chose the spirit of water because it was the element her brother was best at. When it was getting late, everyone headed home.

Olivia was fast asleep on Keith's back, and Keith said to himself, "That was a lot of fun. I can't wait until next year."

CHAPTER 10

The Candidates

On the speakers, President Elaith announced that he had selected five people to be the next president. The candidates were Jord Dunker the troll, Zat Timberland the lizardman, Jasper Richardson the vampire, Ivy Potts the fairy, and Keith Cottam. Everyone in Keith's class looked at him with congrats, but Jord was angry.

After returning home, Keith's friends came over to congratulate him and give him some advice. They told him, "It's not about popularity but magic skills, connecting to people, and how you face a challenge."

The next day, the candidates made posters and gave sweet treats to the other students. Keith and his friends did their part. Keith, Noah, Zosk, and Catherine waved and greeted everyone. Lulu gave everyone her homemade muffins. Olivia was holding a sign that read *Please elect my big brother*. Everyone loved how cute Olivia was holding the sign she'd made.

The candidates were told to assemble in the great hall. Elaith was onstage and told them the tasks to complete. First, they would show how their magic improved. Second, they would test their leadership skills, and finally, they would challenge one of the headmasters.

In the afternoon in the schoolyard, their magic test was about to begin. Zat used his earth magic to make him rock armor. Jasper used water and wind to create ice sculptures of his family. Ivy used water and earth to create a beautiful hawthorn tree. Jord used fire to create giant balls of fire and hit three targets. Keith used water magic and launched a dozen water balls in the sky and created multiple rainbows. The students cheered for their amazing magic.

Two days passed, and the next challenge began. Keith went to a room where three students were waiting for him. The task was to help the three students improve their magic. He talked to them and asked what they were struggling with. He told them to take their time and visualize the element and what they want to do with it. The students of the candidates showed great improvements—all except Jord's.

The final test was upon them, and all of them were on edge. Five of the headmasters were waiting somewhere in the school. The remaining headmasters told them the places to look for them: the garden, training arena, blacksmith room, cafeteria, and the library. Each candidate had to choose one place to go. Zat took the training arena, Jasper took the cafeteria, Ivy took the garden, Jord took the blacksmith class, and Keith took the library. The final test began. It was Zat versus Ugran, Jasper versus Weilt, Ivy versus Horith, Jord versus Krystal, and Keith versus Viktor.

Zat held his ground. Ugran's weapons couldn't lay a scratch on his tough scales. Jasper was having a difficult time; Weilt was evading every attack he threw at him. Ivy was taken down fast. She thought she had the advantage, but Horith used wood magic to take the upper hand. Jord made nonstop attacks, but Krystal took advantage of his anger, and when he lost his strength, she trapped him in an ice prison.

Viktor told Keith, "Your magic has improved, but I will not hold back. So you better fight me like your life depends on it!"

Without warning, a strong wind blasted Keith through a bookshelf. Keith ran to try to catch his breath, but Viktor stopped him. Keith blasted him with water bullets, but Viktor flew up. Then he used wind magic on Keith and flung him around like a rag doll. Keith built a rock dome around himself. He tried to think of his next move, but Viktor kept whaling on him with wind. Keith had to think fast. As the dome broke, Keith was nowhere inside. In a flash, without warning, Keith appeared behind him and launched an attack, but Viktor moved fast and launched a counterattack. Keith vanished without a trace. Viktor looked around, but Keith was nowhere to be seen. Keith appeared out of nowhere again, and his attack almost hit Viktor. Viktor realized that Keith was using shadow teleportation. Like Ash, he could move through the shadows. He was moving like a ninja, waiting for the perfect moment to strike.

Keith used the paper to his advantage, using wind magic to create a paper tornado and trapping Viktor inside. Keith was about to hit him with a rock bullet, but Keith passed out on the floor. Viktor launched an earth spear to hit Keith in the stomach.

As Viktor walked away, he said to Keith, "Don't think just because you were summoned you're all powerful. You still have much to learn." But he turned his head, smiled, and said, "But you showed great passion with your magic. I am proud to be your headmaster."

Keith woke up in the nurse's office with his friends. They told him how amazing he was in his match against Viktor. They said Viktor was top of his class in his old magic school. His preferred element was earth, but he mostly used wind, he only uses earth magic to fight a worthy adversary.

After returning home, Olivia gave Keith a big hug and said, "Welcome home, big brother."

Violet made a big feast to celebrate his performance in his task. After finishing dinner, Keith went straight to bed to be rested up for the big election.

Election Day arrived, and the candidates prepared their final speeches. The candidates' speeches were about themselves or about their families, and now it was Keith's turn. Keith stood in front of the whole student body.

Keith said, "Fellow students, I know I'm not like all of you, but I made great friends and a wonderful little sister here. I want to do my part to make this world—"

Before he could finish that speech, a loud explosion came out of nowhere.

CHAPTER 11

The Dark Undeads

Everyone was scared and confused about that noise. The headmasters and teachers ordered all the students to stay in the great hall. Keith wanted to help, but he didn't know what to do.

Suddenly Keith fell into his shadow. He appeared in a small room with Ash. Keith peeked out of the door and saw a bunch of people with black robes. They captured the teachers and headmasters with some strange dark magic. They entered the great hall and ordered all the students to stay put and quiet. The leader of the group was an elf who pulled out a crystal and held it to his face. A giant reflection of himself appeared on top of the school.

He said, "Greetings, everyone. I am Ahvas, leader of the Dark Undeads. The entire faculty and students are now our hostages. Princess Gemstarzah, all these people will be sacrificed to our Lord Valac unless you give me the fire diamond. You have one hour to deliver the diamond to me."

The reflection disappeared, and the citizens were in a state of worry. The royal council chatted about what to do.

The princess stepped forward and said, "I will not sacrifice innocent lives. I will give the fire diamond to him."

The council did not agree with the princess's decision, but the princess replied, "Well…we better make sure our hero stops him before we arrive."

Back at school, Keith had to think of what he was going to do. Keith used his shadow teleportation to save his friends and come up with a plan. Catherine used her fox, Kitsune, to sense where the enemies and teachers were. Using shadow teleportation, they captured some of the enemies and took their robes to blend in. Keith and Catherine headed to the great hall to save the students, and Lulu, Noah, and Zosk tried to save the teachers. The robes helped them blend in; the enemies didn't suspect a thing. Zosk used his strength to knock out the guards, Lulu stayed with him to offer support, and Noah freed the captive teachers. The students were terrified and worried about what would happen. Ash used his shadow teleportation to transport all the students outside the school. Ahvas looked at Keith and Catherine with anger.

Keith said, "All this for a stupid diamond."

Ahvas laughed and replied, "You fool, it is not just a diamond. It's the diamond of the fire spirit."

Catherine gasped and explained to Keith that the fire diamond was the source of all fire magic. Whoever had the diamond would have the same level of fire magic as the great cosmic spirits. Keith and Catherine had to stop Ahvas. Ahvas launched a giant fireball at them, but Keith created an earth wall, and Catherine jumped in the air and threw two wind blades at him. Ahvas created a giant rock shield and fired lightning at her. She flew out of the way, and Keith entangled him with water tentacles. Using wind, Ahvas blasted out and knocked Keith into the wall. Ahvas tried to hit him with lightning, but Catherine shielded him.

Catherine fell to the ground, and Keith rushed to her with worry and concern on his face. Keith held her as she lay unconscious. Ahvas launched a fireball at him, but he created a wind shield to protect both of them. Keith created an earth dome to keep Catherine safe.

Keith stared at Ahvas and said with anger, "I will not let you hurt anyone ever again."

Ahvas replied, "You are truly powerful but no match for the followers of Lord Valac."

Without warning, Ahvas attacked Keith with a metal whip. Keith dodged it with only a cut on his cheek. He launched a barrage of attacks at him. Keith barely evaded all the attacks until he backed against the wall. The whip turned into flames and was about to hit him, but Ash showed up and saved Keith. With Ahvas distracted, Keith combined his fire and earth magic to create iron fists. Keith blasted off with wind magic, and with his iron fist, he punched Ahvas in the face, launching him out the window so he landed on a fruit stall. Before he passed out, the royal elves surrounded him. The elf princess looked up with a smile, knowing who stopped him. When it was over, Keith rushed to Catherine.

She opened her eyes, and Keith said, "It's ok; we're safe now."

Catherine smiled and leaned closer to Keith; it looked like she was trying to kiss him, but she bit his neck. After sucking Keith's blood, Catherine got her strength and stamina back. All the Dark Undeads were taken by the royal guards.

The day after the attack, Keith and his friends were summoned to the palace. Princess Gemstarzah rewarded them with titles of knights and dames along with one hundred thousand gold coins each. Everyone cheered for their brave deeds.

CHAPTER 12

The Next President

A week after the attack, the school was fully repaired. Everyone assembled in the great hall to see who the next president would be.

President Elaith took the stage and said, "It has been an honor to be your president. I am sad to leave you, but I'm proud that one of these candidates will take my place." After opening the envelope, Elaith said, "And the next president is Keith Cottam."

Everyone clapped and cheered for him. Even three of the candidates congratulated him, but Jord looked angry. Keith shook Elaith's hand and promised to be a great president.

Once he was elected, Keith chose his new student council members. Catherine was the vice president, Noah treasurer, Zosk security, and Lulu was the secretary.

    Keith returned home with exciting news. Olivia gave him a hug, and Violet was preparing a celebratory feast. All his friends enjoyed the meal Violet made for them. After the feast was over, everyone was satisfied with smiles and full bellies. It was late in the night, so Keith decided to let his friends spend the night at his house. The girls took the upstairs, and the boys would sleep downstairs in the living room.

    Lulu came close to Keith and said, "If you want, we can share a bed."

    Keith's face turned red, and Catherine pulled Lulu away by the back of her collar and headed straight to bed.

    In the morning at school, Elaith escorted Keith and his friends to the student council office. A painter was waiting in the room to paint a portrait of him and his council members. Using water magic and watercolors, the portrait was finished in a matter of seconds. Keith was amazed at how good the portrait looked; it was like a photograph in his world.

    A few days passed, and a celebration party was hosted at night to honor Keith for being elected as president. It looked like a school dance. Everyone looked happy and chatted with each other.

Keith thought, *Wow, I came a long way from a normal cashier and a boring life to a magical adventure and savior of the world.*

The musicians asked Keith what to play to honor him. Keith took his MP3 player out and used the speakers in the room to play "Uptown Funk" by Mark Ronson. As soon as it started, everyone started to tap their feet, nod their heads, shake their hips, and the lizardfolks started to slam their tails. Once it picked up, everyone started to dance, and the fairies used their wings to dance in the air. Keith started to dance with his friends, and they all looked happy. Little did they know that in the dark realm, Lord Valac was watching them through a magic mirror.

Lord Valac said, "Enjoy this victory, Keith Cottam. Soon you will regret ever being summoned to that world." He reached out with his finger and tapped the air, and a crack appeared in the air.

The End?

Milton Keynes UK
Ingram Content Group UK Ltd.
UKHW021206291024
450365UK00025B/1174